THE SELTZER MAN

written and illustrated by **Ken Rush**

Macmillan Publishing Company   New York

Maxwell Macmillan Canada   Toronto

Maxwell Macmillan International   New York   Oxford   Singapore   Sydney

First edition
Printed in the United States of America

1   3   5   7   9   10   8   6   4   2

The text of this book is set in 14 pt. Gamma Medium. The illustrations are rendered in oil on panels.

Library of Congress Cataloging-in-Publication Data
Rush, Ken. The seltzer man / written and illustrated by Ken Rush. — 1st ed.   p.   cm. Summary: Two sisters from Brooklyn accompany the seltzer delivery man on what is to be his last delivery. ISBN 0-02-777917-3 [1. Brooklyn (New York, N.Y.) — Fiction. 2. Soft drink industry — Employees — Fiction.] I. Title.
PZ7.R8954Se   1993   [E] — dc20   91-40905

To Eli, of course.

"Eli's coming!" calls my baby sister Beth.

Eli's the seltzer man; he comes to our house once a week to make a delivery.

I sure love seltzer! Not the stuff they sell in the stores, but the old-fashioned kind that comes in heavy glass bottles with the silvery handle and spout on top—the kind Eli delivers.

There's the truck: just as dusty and dented as always, with all those seltzer bottles rattling like crazy.

"You're all bent over, Eli!" Beth cries as he makes his way up the block.

"Oh, Eli, did you hurt your back?" I ask.

"No girls, I'm just plain tired," Eli answers in his nice Brooklyn voice. "Forty years I've been schlepping cases of seltzer. Forty years I've been lifting and carrying, lifting and carrying. I'm sixty years old, girls, and for the first time in my life, I feel all worn out." Eli smiles for us, but I can tell he feels sad inside.

"Now Eli," my mother says from the doorway, "why don't you come in and rest? You can stay for dinner if you like."

I know that will cheer Eli up.

As we finish dinner, Beth asks, "Are you really going to stop being a seltzer man, Eli? Don't you have any more left?"

"Seltzer I got plenty of, sweetheart. I just don't have the energy to deliver it anymore."

"But Eli, if you stop, we'll miss you too much. Who will we have dinner with?"

"I know, sweethearts. My customers are like family to me. I never had any kids of my own. Heck, I never even got married. I was always too busy schlepping seltzer." Eli leans forward in his chair. "I'll visit, ladies, I promise. But there comes a time in life when a person has to make changes. I've made up my mind. This is my last week making deliveries. Old Eli's just too worn-out to be a seltzer man anymore."

We walk out to the truck, and Eli sees how quiet we are.

"Now girls," Eli says in a gentle voice, "don't get upset because of me. I'm just the seltzer man."

Suddenly, Eli's face brightens.

"Why girls, I got an idea! Why don't you two come on a seltzer run with me tomorrow? I'll pick you up early, and we can go to the shop to see how the bubbles and water get put in the bottles. You can meet Georgie—he's the guy who owns the business. He's been working so long that he dreams seltzer dreams at night—counts bottles instead of sheep! Then, we'll make a few deliveries, and you can meet some of my other customers. Whaddya say? You two movie stars want to come on the last seltzer run with the last seltzer man in Brooklyn?"

"You bet we do!"

I dream seltzer dreams all night, just like Georgie the bottle man. I dream that Eli takes us out in his truck, and we drive right up into the sky. We go through clouds of bubbles, and Eli just keeps laughing and laughing.

Eli picks us up early the next morning. He lifts Beth into the truck, but I climb in by myself.

The engine starts with a roar, and we bounce in our seats as the truck leaps forward.

"Off we go!" Eli yells over the rattling of the bottles.

On the way to the seltzer shop, Eli stops the truck to show us the Brooklyn waterfront.

"I always stop here to look at the bridges, ladies." Eli points out each one: the Brooklyn, the Manhattan, and the Williamsburg. "For my money, you can't get a better view of the East River."

The steady hum of the traffic on the bridges mixes with the clanking and clattering of a subway train passing overhead.

When we get to the shop, Eli introduces us to Georgie.

"Eli's told me all about you two," Georgie grins. "I bet you want to see how seltzer is made."

He shows us everything: the bottle-cleaning equipment, the drying racks, and the big green machine that makes the seltzer.

"This tube brings the water in. It gets charcoal-filtered so it's extra pure. And the gas that makes the water bubbly gets pumped in right here." I run my hand over the big, wet machinery. It's really old, but I can tell it's been well taken care of.

"Look Eli, it's magic!" Beth calls as she tries one of the full bottles and squirts seltzer all over the shop.

"Yup," Georgie laughs, "you can tell that's good seltzer because of all the bubbles."

"Come on, ladies," Eli says as we walk out to the truck. "Time for our deliveries."

First we go to Doc Grossman's apartment in Flatbush. She lives in a fancy building, so we can take the seltzer up in the elevator.

Doc Grossman sure is nice to Eli; she treats him like a guest, and treats us to egg creams. She shows us how to make them, with lots of milk, some chocolate syrup, and a couple squirts of seltzer.

"It's kind of a funny name for a drink without any eggs or cream in it," Eli chuckles, "but it's still the best drink for a hot day."

As we finish up, Eli clears his throat and starts to speak. "Now Doc, you know I've been complaining about my back. My truck's worn out, and folks don't want to fuss with my old bottles and crates anymore. I've made up my mind—this is my last seltzer delivery."

"Finish your egg cream, Eli, and don't tell such stories," Doc answers. "I'll see you next week."

As we make each delivery, Eli tells his customers that he's going to retire. Nobody seems to believe him, but Beth and I know he really means it. For the last delivery, we go to an old building in Brighton Beach.

"This is a tough one, girls. Four flights of steep stairs to get to Eddie's apartment. But Eddie's been a customer of mine for years. He really looks forward to my visits 'cause he doesn't get out much anymore."

Eli lightens his load by giving us each a bottle to carry. Even with just one bottle, schlepping seltzer is hard work.

When we leave Eddie's, Eli announces, "That's the last delivery, ladies. Next stop, Coney Island!"

Coney Island means the boardwalk, the beach, the ocean, and all those *rides!* I just love Coney Island. The sounds of the boardwalk mix with the calls of the seabirds. The way the waves bubble and fizzle when they ride up the beach makes them look "just like seltzer," Eli says.

I can smell hot dogs and fries as we approach the snack bar.

"Hey," calls the snack bar man in his long white apron. "It's Eli the seltzer man, and he's got two beautiful girls with him!"

"Hiya, Chief," Eli answers. "Yeah, these are my two new helpers, and I brought them to have lunch on the boardwalk."

"What'll it be, girls?" the Chief asks. "You want some hot dogs, some fries, and maybe a glass of cold seltzer with a squeeze of lemon?"

When we finish eating, I say, "Thanks Eli, this was the best lunch ever."

"That's because you've been schlepping seltzer, and you work up a mighty big appetite carrying all those bottles," Eli answers.

Next, we head to the Wonder Wheel. It's gigantic, and when we start going up, my stomach feels a little funny.

"Look, girls," Eli points, "you can see all of Brooklyn. In my time, I've made deliveries from one end to the other."

Beth's too tired to walk after the ride, so Eli swings her up onto his shoulder.

"Be careful of your sore back, Eli," I tell him.

"Not to worry," Eli grins. "Old Eli feels like he could lift a whole seltzer truck right now. When I'm with you two movie stars, it's like I'm a young man again!"

Eli gently puts Beth in the truck, and I slide in next to her. As we drive home, the tinkling of the bottles sounds like a lullaby. I close my eyes and see my seltzer dream again.

When we get home, Eli carries us up to our front door.

"This was the best run a seltzer man could have," he tells our mom. "The last and the best run ever!"

"Are you sure this has to be your last delivery, Eli?" I ask.

Eli looks at me. His eyes begin to sparkle.

"Well, maybe I got a couple more trips in me yet. After all, if I get too tired, I can always call on my two new helpers."

Eli winks and climbs into his old dented truck.

"See you next week," we call.

As he drives away, he just laughs and laughs and laughs.